The Freaky Joe Club

Other books by P. J. McMahon

The Freaky Joe Club

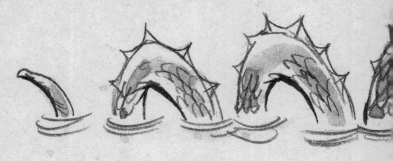

Illustrated by
John Manders

The Freaky Joe Club

Secret File #6:
The Case of the Singing Sea Dragons

by
P. J. McMahon

ALADDIN PAPERBACKS
New York   London   Toronto   Sydney

**For Kathleen Duey, with many thanks,
and for Jane Yolen, who knows why
— P. J. M.**

❧ ALADDIN PAPERBACKS
An imprint of Simon & Schuster Children's Publishing Division
1230 Avenue of the Americas, New York, NY 10020
Text copyright © 2005 by Patricia McMahon
Illustrations copyright © 2005 by John Manders
All rights reserved, including the right of reproduction in whole or in part in any form.
ALADDIN PAPERBACKS and colophon are trademarks of Simon & Schuster, Inc.
Designed by Lisa Vega
The text of this book was set in 14 point Minion.
Manufactured in the United States of America
First Aladdin Paperbacks edition December 2005
10 9 8 7 6 5 4 3 2 1
Library of Congress Control Number 2005923395
ISBN-13: 978-1-4169-0050-4
ISBN-10: 1-4169-0050-0

Table of Contents

Chapter One

All Aboard, All Aboard

On a winter's day in Texas, I sit in The Secret Place of the Freaky Joe Club, holding in my hands the large, red book wrapped all around with a bicycle chain. Yes, the real and true Secret Files of the Freaky Joe Club. As I open the book to write, I am not alone. Riley, the official Beast of our club, lies at my feet chewing a purple dog bone. This seems an odd color to me, but my fellow secret agent Timmy swears purple bones taste good. Riley seems to agree with him.

On a shelf by the window, Bob, our club hamster, lies on a little hamster towel, sunning himself. Who gave him this towel is a mystery I don't have time to solve. But it's surely one of the members of the Freaky Joe Club. Or my little sister. Or her best friend, the evil genius. Or Dwayne, the Silver Streak. Or Mikey, the bug man. This Secret Place is clearly not secret enough. But I can't solve the Mystery of the Silly Hamster Towel because it is time, once again, for me to write. To enter our tale into the Red Book so it becomes part of the Freaky Joe Club history. So those who come after us will learn from our brave adventures. I hope there's enough paper to tell this whole story. Paper . . . hmm. I guess I could say this latest mystery began with a piece of paper. . . .

"Don't you hate it when school starts again after Christmas break? Don't you think winter vacation should be as long as the summer one? Is it me, or is there too much math homework tonight? Why should we have any homework for the first three days after a vacation? What's going on in the library? Why are we standing here?"

Jack, secret agent of the Freaky Joe Club, once again tries to break the record for the number of questions asked in ten seconds.

"Does anyone want some of this?" Timmy asks. He holds a wrinkled bag that looks sort of purple. But maybe it's green. He pulls out something that looks slightly like an orange pumpkin candy from Halloween. And it's January.

"I just had something," I tell him.

"And I don't want to die," Jack announces. "And I still don't know why I'm standing here."

"Because you're waiting with your fellow agents of the Freaky Joe Club to see what strange adventures might happen on a Tuesday afternoon," I suggest to him.

"Great! A mystery! Jack Man is ready! I'll search for clues!" Jack begins to snap his fingers. He runs around, looks under every table and bench, and shouts, "Aha!"

"I thought we're waiting to walk your sister and Mugsy home from school," Timmy says.

"That's what I'm doing," I tell him. "But I don't think that's enough to keep Jack happy."

Jack crawls across the front lobby of the school and rolls under a bench.

"Aha," Timmy says.

"Conor!" Bella yells as the library doors open. She jumps up and down, waving at me. Once again forgetting how to act at school when you see your big brother.

"Conor, we're singing a song about magic animals," she tells me, still jumping up and down. I've got to get my mom to stop putting giant bows in her hair. This one's pink. All the others are pink.

"They're not magical animals, they're disappearing animals," her best friend insists. Mugsy is dressed entirely in brown. I don't know why she's wearing an old-fashioned pilot's helmet. I don't think I want to know.

"They're not disappearing animals, they're endangered animals," Molly McGuire corrects them. Molly is a folk singer who used to be the school custodian, but now is our music teacher. "We're practicing for our Earth Week program. We'll sing songs about all the poor, endangered animals of the world."

"I wanted to be a unicorn," Bella complains. "But I'm a manatee."

"I don't think unicorns are endangered," I tell her. "I think they're gone."

"Probably didn't get enough food," Timmy suggests.

"I'm a Siberian tiger," Mugsy declares, baring her teeth.

"But there'll be no more biting of the other students," Molly reminds her.

"I like the color of your paper, Conor," Bella points at the paper in my hand. I'm holding it so I don't forget to give it to Mom tonight. "Why is there a train on the pink paper?"

"Oh, excellent, it's Imagination Railroad time," Molly says, reading the flyer. "And

this year, you're old enough to compete. You can keep up the family tradition, Conor."

"Family tradition?"

"Your mom? When she went to Edith R. Hammerrocker?" Molly asks these questions as if I know the answer.

I have no idea what she's talking about.

"When your mom went to school here, she was on an Imagination Railroad team. And her team won the championship."

"Cool," Timmy says. Definitely cool.

"Of course, her teammates had a lot to do with it," Molly points out.

"Who were her teammates?" I want to know.

"Why is Jack lying under the table?" Bella wonders.

"He's looking for bad guys," Timmy tells her.

"I'm a good bad guy! Let's get him!" Mugsy roars. Definitely a Siberian tiger.

"Go get him!" Timmy urges.

Mugsy and Bella attack.

"No!" Jack cries when he sees Mugsy coming. He's still upset about the time she tied him up in a tree.

"Stop!" Molly yells. "I told you, Mugsy, you cannot maul any more students."

"Teammates?" I ask.

"Save me!" Jack pleads as he comes out from under the table with Mugsy and Bella attached to him. Bella appears to be singing. Mugsy appears to be chewing on him.

"Check the plaque," Molly tells me. "Jack, stop running or I can't help you."

Jack runs toward the gym with Mugsy still attached. Bella cartwheels after them. Timmy sits on the floor eating more orange things.

"That went well," he says.

"What did she mean by 'check the plaque'?" I ask him.

"Maybe it's on the wall, by Edith and the hamster," Timmy suggests.

"Good detective work," I tell him.

I move on over to the picture of Edith R. Hammerrocker, namesake of our school. Sure enough, the wall is covered in frames. And one of them says:

THIS AWARD IS GIVEN TO THE
EDITH R. HAMMERROCKER ELEMENTARY SCHOOL
TO HONOR ITS HISTORY OF ACHIEVEMENT
IN WINNING THE IMAGINATION RAILROAD
REGIONAL COMPETITION

Then it lists the winning teams, and the year each team won. And there at the top of the list is the Edith R. Hammerrocker Mermaids, a team that consists of Mom, Molly McGuire, Miz

Valerie Barnes from the Big Blue Bookstore, and two other names. Well, it makes sense that they would be on the same team. I know, and now Timmy and Jack know, that the Mermaids had been working together under another name.

I check out the names of the other teams. And notice it's been a while since our school won. Maybe it's time for our school to win again. I think this Freaky Joe Club is about to take on the job.

"Let's do this, Timmy," I call over to him. "Let's have a team, and win."

"Win what?" Timmy stops eating and heads my way.

"Yeah, win what, Hamster Man?"

I hate that name.

Jeremiah and Jake, of the Sylvan Glen Sharks swim team, and hockey team, and baseball team, and Any Other Sport That Is Played in the Universe team, look over my shoulder at the list.

"Just the Imagination Railroad competition. Nothing you'd be interested in."

"What makes you so sure?" Jeremiah asks.

"Yeah," says Jake.

"Just am," I say.

"You are?" Timmy asks me.

"Sure," I tell him.

"Well, the Sharks can beat you guys in any competition." Jeremiah sticks his face way too close to mine.

"Not this one," I tell them.

"Oh yeah?" Jake says. He has such a way with words.

"Oh yeah," I promise.

"We'll see about that," Jeremiah says. "Come on, Jake, we need to sign up our team. We'll see you at the winner's circle. We'll be in it, and you'll be watching."

"Yeah," Jake adds, walking away backward.

Which means he falls over Jack, who is crawling with Mugsy on his back.

"Did that go well?" Timmy asks.

I have no idea.

Chapter Two
Yes, Jack, It's a Straw

"Why were you talking to the Sharks?" Jack asks. "Aren't they supposed to be our enemies?"

"I thought your enemy was a sweet little girl with curly red hair," Timmy tells him.

"Sweet? Sweet? Genghis Khan wants to be her when he grows up." Jack shakes his whole body, then snaps his fingers. "Okay, what are we looking at? Why are we standing here?"

"We were looking at you crawl down the hall," Timmy tells him.

"You'd crawl too, if you had a maniac on your back." Jack insists. "How about I jump on your back, Pumpkin Boy, and see how you like it."

"How about you don't," Molly orders as she comes up behind me. She has Mugsy under one arm and Bella under another.

"Our school hasn't won in a long time," I mention.

"So, are you the team to change that?" Molly asks.

"We need five kids and a coach," I reply, checking the pink paper.

"I count three right here." Molly points with her chin, as her hands are still full of singing, endangered animals.

"I could find two more," I tell her.

"We could add two more Bullfrogs," Timmy suggests.

"That'd be five," I agree.

"Are we doing math homework?" Jack asks.

The very next afternoon, our new team meets in the Secret Place. Murphy and Mad Dog, the other members of our Bullfrog hockey team, have signed on. As Murphy has the bad luck to be Mugsy's older sister, I think she's happy to do anything that doesn't involve babysitting.

"All right, team. We are about to begin our ride on the Imagination Railroad." Molly is wearing blue overalls and an old-fashioned trainman's hat. "It may be a long, hard journey, but good times will surely be waiting at the end."

Did I mention our coach also writes folk songs?

"You have your coach"—Molly bows to us—"and your assistant coach ready, willing, and able to help you."

My mom, covered in green paint, waves a paintbrush at us. A few drops spatter, leaving Bob the Hamster to wonder why there's green rain today.

"Exactly what is the Imagination Railroad?" Murphy asks.

"And do we have to talk funny and wear goofy clothes?" Jack wants to know.

"Think of it this way," Molly suggests. "You win a baseball game if you have good hitters, runners, and catchers on your team. You win a basketball tournament if you can jump higher and shoot baskets better than anyone else. A hockey team wins if it can skate faster and score more goals. An Imagination Railroad team wins if it has the best brains: kids who can think fast and have creative and interesting minds."

"Huh?" Jack asks.

"But where's the train?" Mad Dog wants to know.

"We're in trouble," Timmy says.

"We're not in trouble," Molly tells us. "To win, a team needs to have a real mix—have really different kinds of kids."

So we have that part covered.

"There are two parts to the competition," Mom jumps in. "The Quick Round and the Play."

"Only four players are in the Quick Round," Molly explains, "so if you have a player who's not good at that part, he or she can sit it out."

"I'm confused," Jack moans.

"Can you be on the team if you have no brain?" Timmy asks. He pounds on Jack's head, listening for a sound.

"We'll do a Quick Round. You'll get it." Molly grabs Jack just as he's about to pounce like a Siberian tiger. "Line up behind Bob's table."

Bob waves his fist at us when Mom moves his house to the floor.

Molly sets a timer on the table and lays down two straws. "In the Quick Round, the judge will give you something, like these straws. And you have a minute to show how many different, creative ways you can think about it."

"Watch." Mom picks up the straws, holds them behind her head. "Reindeer." She passes them quickly to Molly. Who picks them up, holds them in front of her eyes and says, "binoculars."

"Cool, I like this." Timmy takes

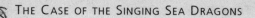

the straws, holds them near his mouth. "Walrus."

"Way to go," Molly says. "Pass them to the next person, fast."

Murphy takes the straws, frowns, and holds them between her fingers, across one palm. "Chopsticks."

Mad Dog holds them out in front of him, moving them back and forth. "I'm looking for water."

"Yes," Molly shouts. "You guys have got it."

Mad Dog passes me the straws. I hold them on each side of my neck. "Robot."

Jack gets the straws. Stares at them.

Looks worried at us. Holds them near his mouth. "Straws?" he says.

"If you don't have an idea, pass the straws on," Mom tells us. "Every player gets a point for each of his or her ideas. Then the individual scores are added up for the team score."

"Sometimes one person is better at this than another. It's like your lead-off batter. You keep passing to that person," Molly explains.

Timmy holds the straws together. "Fetch, dog," he says, pretending to throw. Riley runs after it, barking.

Holding them together, Murphy waves them in the air. "Conductor in the orchestra."

"Javelin," Mad Dog calls as he pretends to throw

them across the
room.

I lay them on
the table, crossed.

"Here lies the treasure," I say.

Jack takes the straws. Sips. "Straws?" he says.

Molly takes them away. "You guys are going to
be a great team. You really have the idea."

"Straws?" Jack asks.

"Some of us have the idea,"
Timmy says.

"Jack'll be fine," Mom assures
us.

"They're doing some-
thing with straws."

Who said that?

"Did anyone hear anything?" I ask.

"Just the sound of Jack thinking," Timmy says.

"Can you see the straws?"

"Either we have a ghost, or someone's outside," I say.

Crash.

"That's my bicycle," Jack says.

"That's our ghost!" I yell as I run out the door.

Chapter Three

JUST What Is a LUderino?

As fast as I can, I run outside. Some bicycles stand up alongside the Secret Place. One or two lie on the ground, knocked over. Knocked over by someone making a getaway?

Who was listening outside the Secret Place?

I run to the front of the garage, looking to catch that someone running away. But there's no one there.

"My bike, my bike!" Jack runs around yelling.

"It's right here, dear," Mom tries to tell him. But Jack keeps going.

"Timmy, check the back gate," I call. Bad guys have been known to use our back gate.

"No one back here," he reports.

"Here's my bike," Jack says. He hugs it.

"Are you sure you heard something?" Mom asks. "Riley didn't bark to say anyone was there."

"Oh," Timmy says. "Maybe she was too busy eating the Most Amazing Giant Dog Biscuit that I gave her."

"Bicycles fall over all the time," Molly points out.

"Not my bicycle," Jack says.

"It loves Jack and would never fall over," Timmy tells us.

"Someone said 'They're doing something with straws' just before the crash," I insist.

"Someone was spying on us," Murphy says.

"Why would someone do that?" Mad Dog asks.

"Because they think we're the best, and we're going to win, and they want to know how we are going to do it?" I answer. I mean, why else?

"Or it could just be someone acting goofy," Mom says as she waves her paintbrush all around.

"Let's just go back and practice, and not worry about it," Molly suggests.

We shuffle back into the Secret Place. Where we find Riley happily sleeping on her back, her stomach full of Giant Dog Biscuit.

• • • •

"Where are we going, anyway? Is this meeting tonight about straws?" Jack asks for the third time.

"No, Jack, we're just going to an information session," Molly promises him. Again. Our new Imagination Railroad team is packed into my mom's truck. Which still has SWAMP MOBILE written on the side. In glow-in-the-dark green paint.

"What I love about the Imagination Railroad," Molly tells us, "is that it's all about using your mind. There's no big fuss, no silliness, just kids coming together to use their imaginations."

"This is the place, right?" Mom asks Molly as she pulls up in front of a big school.

"Isaure Moorehead High School." Molly checks the name on the school against her paper. "This is it."

Just then a line of kids walks past us. Each has a hand on the shoulder of the kid in front. They march, singing:

"We've been riding on the railroad,
all the livelong day
"We've been riding on the railroad,
'cause we're smart, hooray!"

We stare.

"Kinda weird," Timmy announces.

No silliness, I wonder?

"Well," Mom says, "there's always one in every crowd."

"One what?" I ask.

"Let's just go to this meeting," Molly says. "We'll find out about the Play, rules and regs, the whole shebang."

"What's a shebang?" Jack asks.

"I think it's a kind of ice-cream sundae," Timmy says.

The gym at the Moorehead High School is filled with Imagination Railroad teams and their coaches. Some of the teams wear matching shirts. Some are wearing matching hats. Even more appear to be dressed in costumes. I don't know why, but there is one group of kids who are all wearing Viking helmets. With horns. Lots of the groups are singing. Or chanting. One bunch of kids is chanting and clapping.

"Kinda very weird," Timmy says.

"Kinda time to go home," Jack insists.

"This is odd," Mom says.

"It seems to have changed," Molly admits. "Not to worry, we'll be fine."

"There's a place over there to sign in," I tell her.

"Forward ho, team." Molly points the way.

"Forward ho! Forward ho! Forward ho!" Jack chants loudly as we walk across the gym.

"Stop that, Jack," seven people tell him.

"Nice hat," Molly tells the lady behind the desk who wears an old-fashioned trainman's hat. "I've got the same one."

"I don't think so. This is an official Imagination Railroad hat." The lady shows her the two large red words. "Only those of us who always ride the train are allowed to have them."

"Mondo weird," Timmy whispers. Loudly.

"We're here to sign up." Molly ignores the hat stuff. "What do I do?"

"This is where coaches register their teams, their team names, and the names of the team members." The lady hands her a clipboard.

"Guys, we have a problem," Molly tells us. "We forgot to choose our name."

"Can't we just be the Edith R. Hammerrocker team?" Murphy asks.

"But there's another team from your school, dearie," the hat lady tells us. "They just signed in." The lady points across the room.

Jeremiah, Jake, Mick, and two other guys wave at us. Well, they don't wave exactly. They move their hands, sort of. Not in a friendly way. They're wearing baseball hats with sharks' heads coming out the front. Sharks that have big, wide-open mouths full of giant teeth. Big

Buster, the hockey coach, is with them.

"What name will you use? We need to hurry and sign you in. The Luderino will be here very soon," this strange lady tells us.

"What the heck is a Luderino?" Mom asks. She looks like she's getting cranky. Which is not good.

"Excuse us a minute, please," Molly says. "Team meeting over by the water fountain."

"I am not wearing horns on my head," Mad Dog announces.

"Good decision," Molly tells him. "Ignore these show-offs. I don't know why they have all this silly stuff. But we need a name."

Mad Dog offers the name of our swim team. "Octopi?"

"I think we should have a

special name just for this team. Like Valerie, Conor's mom, and I were the Mermaids."

"I think a sea name, like Mermaid," Murphy suggests.

"I'm not dressing up like a mermaid," Jack declares. "It's hard to walk in fins."

"We're not dressing up, that's not what this is about," Mom insists.

"Something different," Molly suggests. "A name no one else will have."

"Conor will know something," Timmy says.

The team turns to me. In my mind, I turn the pages of *The Big Book of Undersea Life*, which is an important book in the history of the Freaky Joe Club.

Something different . . . something unusual . . . something no one else will have . . . something that's hard to find . . . I've got it!

"Sea Dragons!" I announce. "The Hammer-rocker Sea Dragons."

"Dragons are good," Jack says. "Dragons are fierce."

"Real creature?" Molly asks.

"Yup. One of the rarest," I tell her.

"I'm liking it," Timmy says.

"Anyone opposed?" Molly asks. "By your silence, I hereby declare you the Sea Dragons." She scoots over to the sign-in table. As a group, we scoot too.

"The Hammerrocker Sea Dragons are good to go." Molly signs the form.

"And just in time. Find a seat. We're about to start." The railroad hat lady shoos us to the floor. "The Luderino is here."

Chapter Four

Now, What Is a Winkledorf?

The Hammerrocker Sea Dragons crowd into a spot on the floor. Right next to the gang of Vikings.

"Excuse me." Molly taps the largest Viking on the shoulder. "I'm a little confused. What is a Luderino?"

"Not what, but who," the Viking answers. "She's the head of the Imagination Railroad for all the western regions."

"Why do they call her the Luderino?"

"Sometimes they call me the Jack," Jack points out. "But that has to do with a poop bug."

"Is the Luderino a type of bug?" Mad Dog asks.

"I don't think you should say that," the Viking tells us. "If you want to ride the railroad, you have to respect *the* conductor. *The* Luderino. She can make or break a team."

"That doesn't make any sense," Mom tells him.

"But why are you wearing horns on your head?" Jack asks. "What has that got to do with a railroad?"

"We are Vikings of the Rakonaard people," the man tells us. "We always set our plays in the time of the Vikings. The horns will help us to win. The Luderino likes to see enthusiasm," he adds. "And Chandler T. LeFlore is the Viking to do it."

"Okay, mondo weird," we all say at the same time.

"Look, there she is." The horned man points his finger across the gym.

A very tall woman talks to the strange sign-up lady with the trainman's hat. A very tall, movie star kind of lady. She has long blonde hair, fancy clothes, fancy high heels, fancy jewelry. A fur scarf goes around her shoulders. Picking up some papers, she moves to the front of the room.

"Did she know this meeting was going to be in a gym?" Molly asks.

"I always wear my leopard suit when I go to meetings in a gym," Mom tells her.

This sentence seems very funny to Molly, who laughs loudly.

"I like to wear my pink, fluffy one," Molly adds.

Which makes my Mom laugh even louder.

Which, of course, makes people look at us.

Which makes me want to wear a sign saying THAT WOMAN IS NOT MY MOTHER.

The Luderino looks over. And she doesn't look happy.

Mom and Molly are too busy laughing to notice, or they would see the tall woman's face. She looks shocked. I watch as she points Mom and Molly out to the hat lady. Who writes something on a piece of paper and hands it to her. Which makes the Luderino look even more surprised.

"I think you should stop laughing," I suggest.

"The Luderino might not like it," the Viking says.

"Oh, please," Mom tells him.

"I don't think she does," I say.

The Viking moves away from us on the floor.

The tall lady moves to the front of the crowd. Which bursts into applause.

"Welcome, railroad riders, welcome." The lady puts her arms out to the side, making little circles with her hands. "Another grand competition is upon us. Some of you have ridden my railroad before; some of you are new. All of you will meet the challenge of these games. This I know."

"Her railroad?" Molly asks out loud.

"Can I ask her why everyone is looking pretty strange?" Jack whispers loudly.

"Is someone speaking at the same time as I

am?" The lady puts her hand to her heart, as if she can't believe this is possible.

"Oh no, Luderino," cries a lady who appears to have a large frog on her head.

The fancy lady stares at our group.

"For those of you who may not know me," she begins, "I am Ralfaella Luderino, and I have the great honor of heading this Imagination Railroad. Tonight I will review a few rules, remind you of a few important dates, and tell you about some important awards. Then I will answer any questions you may wish to ask of me."

She reads from one of her papers. "In this year's play, you will bring an inanimate object to life. You will give life to that which has none, for a reason. And you will celebrate the occasion with an original song. Anyone imitating Elvis will be asked to leave the contest."

She begins to read off the dates that the coaches must remember. Molly scribbles on her notepad. My mind races ahead. What object should we bring to life?

"Wilhelmina Winkledorf. Remember her name," the Luderino tells us.

"Who could forget it?" Mom elbows Molly.

"She was the most creative player ever to do the Quick Round. There was no thinker like her. And so the Wilhelmina Winkledorf Award is given—not every time, oh no—but whenever a railroad rider is so original, so creative, so free in thinking in new directions that he or she must be noted. And the Winkledorf prize brings many points to the winning team. Points that can make the difference between losing or advancing to the next round. Remember, teams win the World Series or take home the Stanley Cup based on the hard work and creative thinking of each and every player. And I will be watching you; I will be looking for those players I can reward."

"You know, it's weird, but I feel like I know this Luderino person," Molly says.

"Ditto," says Mom.

"Shh," say the Viking Man and the Frog Lady at the same time.

"Is there a problem?" the Luderino asks.

"Nope," Molly answers.

"Do you need my help?"

"Nope."

"We can always use your help," the Viking calls out.

Molly gives the guy a look. "Why do you keep doing that?"

"Being nice to her is always good for points," he

whispers. "It can make the difference between winning or not."

"Don't be silly," Molly tells him. She turns to us. "Kids, you win or lose on how creative a team you are, on how you work together."

The Viking rolls his eyes at Molly. "Oh please."

The Luderino stands with her arms crossed, tapping her foot. "I would like to go on. As some new teams have joined us tonight, I thought we might have a sample Quick Round. Young man with the shark hat, could you come up?"

Jeremiah runs to the front.

"And the girl with the lovely pyramid on your head, yes you, and the Mayan princess. Great, and one more." Luderino swivels around, pointing at me. "And the young man with the red hair."

"I wouldn't go if I were you, Conor," Jack says.

"Go on, sweetie, you'll do fine." Mom pats me on the shoulder.

I head to the front.

"Line up, line up." I end up next to Jake, as she pushes us around. She ends up dropping her pile of papers. Rushing to pick them up first, the Pyramid knocks over the Princess.

"Here you are, ma'am."

"Thank you. Now, everyone, take your places behind the table here. The timer is set." She hands the first girl a long piece of red licorice. "And go!"

The girl wraps it across her shoulders. "Feather boa."

"Bracelet," says the next, passing it quickly.

Jeremiah looks at it. Says nothing.

"Pass it!" hisses the pyramid.

I grab it from Jeremiah. He keeps a tiny bit. I hold it up, measure the air, squint and say "Six inches long." I pass it.

"Jump rope!"

"Spaghetti!"

Jeremiah just looks at it.

It's a little shorter when I get it. I hold it away from me, wrestling with it. I fall to the ground, yelling "Man-eating snake!"

I come up, hand it to the Pyramid. And head back down to pick up a piece of paper under the table. Just as the buzzer rings.

And loud applause follows.

"Way to go, Snake Boy!" Molly yells.

"Well. Wasn't that interesting?" Ralfaella Luderino makes little fake claps with her hands.

Not as interesting as the paper I found—with the words HER NAME IS MOLLY MCGUIRE written on it.

Chapter Five

The Kingdom of the Dump

The Freaky Joe Club + Mad Dog + Murphy + one head coach + one assistant purple-colored coach are assembled and ready. Large pieces of white paper hang on the wall, waiting for clues. Markers are ready to write them down. Books are nearby. All systems are go.

"Do we have to write a whole play?" Jack

moans, rolling on the floor. "Isn't that like a giant home-work assignment?"

"What kind of object was she talking about?" Mad Dog wants to know.

"It's a good thing I have a big bag of candy to keep us going," Timmy tells us, holding up a large, brown, crumpled, ripped bag with the words GERBIL FOOD on the side.

I write in big letters:

WHERE ARE WE?

WHAT DO WE BRING TO LIFE? WHY?

"Good, Conor," our coach tells us. "Guys, don't worry about silly people in horns or people who overdress for a small meeting at the gym. This is going to be fun. And you're going to be good at it. Conor did great last night."

"Snake Boy, Snake Boy!" my team chants.

Bob the Hamster looks alarmed. And dives under his wood chips.

"And Jeremiah was soooo bad," Jack says happily.

"Attention, team. This is your coach speaking. You need to think of this as telling a story. There is a group of people that brings something to life. For a reason. Let's throw out some answers. Where are these guys?"

"A lake."

"A mountain."

"A forest."

"More interesting," Mom says as Molly writes.

"The circus," I say.

"A bakery," Timmy suggests.

"The dump," Jack calls from the floor.

The dump? A dump!

"That's really good," I say. "There's a lot of stuff in the dump."

"I like it," Murphy says. Mad Dog nods.

"You do?" Timmy asks.

"You do!" Jack says, jumping up. "Jack Man is on the playwriting job."

"We're in a dump. Who are all of you?" Molly asks.

"Crazy people who live in a dump," Murphy says.

"Because we like it there," Timmy adds.

"Because we think it's great," I suggest. "We think it's the Kingdom of the Dump!"

"Yeah!" Timmy yells. "We all live in the Kingdom of the Dump. I'm a crazy chef who loves to cook from all the food there."

"What is it that you bring to life?" Molly asks. "Is it something you find there?"

"A statue," Mad Dog says. "We find a statue and bring it to life."

Good, this is good. A lot of *yeah*s from the team.

"Great story you have going here," Molly tells us. "What is it a statue of?"

"Not what, who!" I shout.

"Who is it?"

Silence.

Who's in the dump? A statue, a statue. My

favorite knight detective, Sir Chester the Clever, pops into my brain. Sir Chester fighting for his . . .

"The king!" I announce. "It's a statue of the king."

More *yeah*s.

"Which king?" our coach wants to know.

"King Bob," Timmy says.

"Good King Bob," Murphy adds.

"There's a statue of King Bob in the Kingdom of the Dump," Mad Dog sums it up.

"Why?" Molly holds the pen, ready to write.

"Why? Why? Why?" Jack paces, snapping his fingers. "Why am I in the dump?"

"Because, because . . . ," I answer. "Because a bad wizard has turned Good King Bob into a statue, and taken over the country, and ordered all the statues in the kingdom removed. This one is the real Good King Bob. If we bring him back to life, he can save the country."

"We can all save the country," Murphy says.

"Who says Jack is Good King Bob?" Timmy wants to know.

"Good, good, good, good, good." Molly laughs while she's writing. Mom gives me a thumbs-up. "And what song do you sing?"

"The Good King Bob song?" Jack suggests.

"The dinner song?" Timmy thinks.

"The dump song?" Mad Dog shrugs his shoulders.

"Yes, the song of the dump," Murphy says.

"Yeah," I agree. "The national anthem of the Kingdom of the Dump."

"Oh yeah," Molly says. "I think we have a go. Let's get this script written."

"We're not done?" Jack asks. "We've got home-work?"

"Good King Bob," I tell him, "we have to know how we shall bring you to life."

"Yes, of course, proceed," Jack says, standing up straight and tall.

"Huh?" we all say at the same time.

The Imagination Railroad may be a fun road to ride, but it's also a lot of work. In competition, we have eight minutes to move onto a blank floor or stage, set up the scene with all our props, and perform our play. Minutes over count against our score.

"I'm getting sick of our song," Mad Dog says one day. I can see his point. We've sung it ten times today.

"You're still two minutes over," Molly says, looking at her stopwatch. "You've got to get it down."

"I can say 'Look, his hand,' Murphy suggests, "instead of 'What doth my love have in his goodly hand?'"

"Much better," Jack says. Everyone thought it was a great idea that Murphy would be a crazy lady who thinks Good King Bob is her boyfriend. Everyone except Jack, that is.

"We'll go through it one more time. Then we'll do one Quick Round and call it a day."

"Yes!" Jack and Mad Dog pump their hands in the air.

"You don't practice for this any more than you do for baseball or hockey," Molly points out.

"Yes, but in baseball I get to run around. Here I have to stand still for a looooonnnnnggg time,"

Jack protests. He makes a good King Bob, but it's hard for Jack to be frozen as a statue.

"We have to decide today who will be in our Quick Round," Molly says, reading from her thick pile of Imagination Railroad papers. "All five teammates must be in the Play or you're disqualified, but only four can be in the Quick Round."

"There are a lot of complicated rules in this game," Mad Dog says.

"I know," Molly says. "It reminds me of the infield fly rule in baseball."

"How will we decide?" I ask. I'm pretty sure who we don't want in the Quick Round. In all our practices, Jack has never said anything but "Straw?"

"Maybe really bad people shouldn't play?" Timmy suggests.

"You're all great," Molly says. Molly lies. "But I have to say, Jack, I'm worried. You have such an important role as Good King Bob. Maybe you should use the Quick Round to prepare yourself—a bit like being in the on-deck circle."

"And since coaches aren't allowed in the Quick Round room," Mom adds, "Molly and I could give you special coaching."

I decide to help. "You know, Jack, every team has to protect its best players. You don't send your best pitcher out until the biggest game."

"I simply have to agree. I shall sit out the Quick Round for the good of my kingdom." Jack is standing up straight again.

"I think you have made a noble decision," the coach tells him.

"A king's duty is to serve his people," Jack answers.

"I think his body has been taken over by pod people," Timmy says. "They've taken our Jack and left us someone who can talk."

"They're talking about pod people," a voice says. "I think they're doing something in space."

This time Riley barks. And runs. Over to the window, where she stands on her hind legs, barking louder than loud.

I run out the door. Run around the garage. Run to the back of the house. No one. How are they getting away? And who are they?

And what is it they want to know?

Chapter Six

Ride a Swamp Mobile to Meet the Aliens

"Are you sure you won't be arrested for driving like this?" I yawn and ask my Mom the question at the same time.

"This isn't any worse than the Swamp Mobile," she says. "And that was never a problem."

Not a problem? Driving around with a large bullfrog head on the top of our truck? But that was better than the collection of garbage that is there now. Nice-looking garbage, which has been nicely painted in colors, but still garbage.

Not to mention the large signs on both sides. Signs saying OFFICIAL ROYAL CARRIAGE OF KING BOB and ALL HAIL THE KINGDOM OF THE DUMP!

"I'm just trying to support you, sweetie," Mom says. "I think the play is great. The team does swell together. And you are one of the finest Quick Round players I have ever seen."

"Really?"

"Truly. And this is coming from one of the best Quick Round players I ever met." Mom pats herself on the back. "If I do say so myself. There was only one player better than me."

"Too bad we can't ask Wilhelmina Winkledorf what she thinks," I say.

"She was the only one better than me," Mom says. "And she was a much better sport than Ralphie."

"You know her? And who's this Ralphie guy?" I ask.

"Yup, I rode the railroad at the same time as Wilhelmina. I'll tell you some other time. But right now we've got to go and pick up the others." Mom jumps into the car. "Can't be late, you know. That's points off."

"We could pretend we like that Luderino lady, and we'd get them back," I say.

"Conor!" My mom sounds shocked.

"I was joking," I tell her. "Why does she get to do that anyway?"

"I'm not sure she does," Mom says. "Somebody got that silly idea once, and now everyone believes it. That's what I think."

I'm not so sure that's what I think.

But I am sure that space aliens landing on Earth today at the Chloe Lauren Middle School would take one quick look around and leave. "Earthlings are crazy people. Let's try another planet."

The Vikings are here. And a group of kids who appear to be dressed as a moose herd. Wizards go by, and a troop of life-size, green plastic army men. Kids are marching with their hands on one another's shoulders, marching in a line, walking in herds mooing. Carrying large boxes filled with strange stuff.

"I wonder if we'll lose points for just wearing our t-shirts," Murphy says.

Mom made us bright yellow shirts with a painting of a sea dragon swimming. Bright coral and sea plants are all around. It's a good team shirt.

"You don't lose points for how you're dressed. And it's better to wear a team shirt, not a costume, during Quick Round. Costumes are distracting," Molly reminds us. "And you won't know till you get inside which you'll do first."

"Let's get the dump inside," Mom suggests.

Armed with black garbage bags, cardboard boxes, a wagon, and a clothesline, we head inside to ride this railroad.

"Here's the deal. You do your play first, in one hour. Then you have a break, with time for lunch. You're in the last Quick Round. The Play is in the gym. Quick Round is in room one thirteen."

Reading over her shoulder, I notice something interesting. We go on soon after the Sharks.

With only a little time to go, and with our costumes and props ready, we watch the dreaded Sharks compete.

The stage area is marked on the floor with masking tape. Two judges sit behind a table, ringing a bell to say the timer has started. The team runs out, sets up the scene, and goes.

The Sharks seem a little disorganized. Four of them wear some kind of antennae, which keep falling off. Their costumes seem to be made of aluminum foil wrapped all around them. And it keeps ripping.

"Do you think they're silver mummies?" Murphy asks.

"I don't remember mummies having antennae," Timmy says.

"Maybe they're giant silver bugs," Mad Dog suggests.

"I think they're space mummies," Jack says. "Space people usually have antennae, but don't have vowels in their names."

Space people? What was it the voice outside my window said: "I think they're doing something in space"?

Are the Sharks spying on us? And copying us?

What do they think will happen if they do?

Here's what actually happens when the bell rings. The aluminum foil mummies run out into the square. They place a tiny toy spaceship on the floor next to them. Jake, who is not wrapped, lies down on the floor. The mummies crouch down next to the tiny spaceship. They leap up.

"We made it!" they yell.

"Greetings, earthling," they say.

Jake doesn't move.

"What is wrong with the earthling?" Jeremiah asks.

"He must be inanimate," Mick says.

"Let us make him come alive," Jeremiah says.

They stand in a circle around him. Jump up and down. Sing the words "Oh, don't be dead, oh, don't be dead."

Jake sits up. "Oh, I'm not dead anymore. I thank you."

"Why did we save him?" asks a Shark whose aluminum foil is down around his ankles.

"Because it is better

to be alive than dead," Jeremiah answers. He turns to the judges. "The End."

"Okay, I'm so not worried anymore," Murphy tells me.

The room is silent. The judges' mouths hang open. The only sound is Big Buster clapping and giving a big, two-finger whistle.

Finally one of the judges finds her voice. "Thank you for the most . . . unusual play I have ever seen," she says.

Jeremiah kicks the spaceship off the floor. That must surely count for points off.

Next, we watch the Vikings try to bring a yak back to life so their children won't go hungry in the cold winter.

"I didn't know yaks lived near the Vikings," Molly says.

"They don't," I tell her. I've read *Animals of the World, Volume III.*

Then we're on. Holding our bags and boxes, we say softly, "Sea Dragons rule, the ones who go to Edith's old school."

The bell rings. We run. With bags, and boxes, and broken-down toys, with a clothesline covered with funny old shorts, with buckets and brooms and a busted basket of books, we create the Kingdom of the Dump. Those of us who live there wear funny old clothes. Jack wears all the old knight's armor I used to dress up in. His face is painted gray and a helmet covers his head.

Mad Dog pulls a wagon into the dump. "Hey, look what I found," he says. And our play begins. Murphy finds the secret note in the statue's hand, which tells what has happened and gives a hint of how we can reverse the spell. We do it, and Good King Bob convinces us to follow him on a march to free the nation. We head off, circling the dump, singing our song that ends:

Yes, have you seen the
kingdom of the Dump?
Underwear, underwear

everywhere, we do love the kingdom of
the Dump, Plenty, plenty here to share.

And we're done. Molly and Mom jump up and down. We must be under our time! And what's that sound? Clapping. The judges and the other kids and coaches are clapping for our team.

"Yes!" we shout. We high-five each other.

"Sea Dragons rule!" Mom shouts.

"Sea Dragons rule?" Jeremiah says, coming up alongside me. "I guess you think your play was pretty good?"

I have to admit it. "Our play was pretty good," I tell him.

Jake fumbles over to us, foil falling off him. "You think that was good, Hamster Boy?"

"It *was* good," Jeremiah tells him.

"Huh?" Jake says.

Huh?

Before I can say anything, Jeremiah and Jake and the aluminum foil are gone.

"On to the Quick Round," Molly tells us.

"I thought you said we had lunch first," Timmy says in a worried voice.

Chapter Seven

Hello? Hello? Anyone There?

"You know," Jack says, "I was so good, I could be in the Quick Round."

"You were all great," Mom says. "You might be first in this round."

"If the Quick Round goes well, we are a definite for regional," Molly promises.

The Luderino walks through the cafeteria, wearing a fancy red suit and red high, high heels. Everyone tries to get her attention. Everyone, except our team. And she heads straight over to us.

"I hear from the judges that your play was well done," she says. "And well coached," she adds, looking Mom and Molly slowly in the eyes.

She turns away, moving slowly through the cafeteria, making little hand waves as she goes.

"Do we know her?" Mom asks Molly.

"I keep thinking she looks familiar," Molly tells Mom.

"Familiar, but not familiar, if you know what I mean?" Mom says.

"I know exactly what you mean," Molly assures her.

"I have no idea what you're talking about," I tell them both. "But I keep forgetting to tell you, that lady had a piece of paper with Molly's name on it."

"What's wrong with that?" Mom asks.

"It was at the first meeting. I found it under the table. It must mean something," I insist.

"I think you shouldn't worry about that," Molly says.

"I think I need more food," Timmy says.

"Fifteen minutes till Quick Round," Mom reminds him. "So finish up."

A girl dressed as a green army man comes running up. "I'm helping pass out notes to all the teams," she says. "You're the Sea Dragons, aren't you?"

"That's us," I tell her.

"Here's your note." She hands me an envelope.

"What's it about?"

"I don't know, I'm just handing envelopes to teams. I think it might help me get some extra points for my team." She runs off in the direction of the moose herd.

I pull a piece of paper from the envelope. "There's a team captain meeting in the library."

"When?" Mom asks.

"Right now."

"I didn't know we needed a captain. What should we do?" Molly asks us. "We have our Quick Round coming up."

Timmy points at his mouth and the two pieces of pizza on his plate.

Jack and Mad Dog are busy running up and down the sides of the cafeteria.

"I vote for Conor," Murphy says.

Molly looks at me. "Okay?"

It's okay with me.

"You have to hurry back here, or meet us at room one thirteen. We need you," Mom says.

"It's you or Jack," Timmy reminds me.

"I'll meet you at the room," I promise.

"Take this map of the school." Molly hands me a folded piece of paper. "Room one thirteen."

I hurry to the library. This had better be a short meeting. The first door I try is locked. Down the hall, I see the sign: TEAM CAPTAINS MEETING. Oh man, I am going to have to rush to get to our Quick Round. I hurry in, pushing the door hard. The door slams behind me. "Sorry," I say. To the AV carts, and the shelves of slide projectors, and brown boxes labeled BOOKS. Lots of stuff. No other kids. No team captains, no other riders on the Imagination Railroad.

"Okay, not the right room," I admit to the overhead projector next to me. The Sea Dragons will have to skip the meeting. I am heading for Quick Round.

I am pulling on the door. I am pulling harder and harder. And the door is staying put. Which is bad. Really bad. I pull harder, and harder. Nothing. This is really, really bad! So I do the sensible thing.

"Help! Help! I'm locked in this room!"

Someone has to hear me—the team captains are meeting somewhere nearby.

An awful thought sneaks in the back corner of my brain: What if the team captains are not meeting nearby? What if this is a trap? A trap to catch a Conor?

Okay, that works to calm me down. I mean, why would anyone want to do that? All that's going to happen is that I'm going to miss the Quick Round. Which is really, really bad! 'Cause I'm pretty good at it. And Jack is pretty terrible.

"Hello, hello, hello, HELLO! HELLO!" I bang on the door. No one comes. So I kick the door. I think the school librarian would definitely not like this. But she's not locked in. I am. So I kick really, really hard. So hard I fall flat on my back. And no one comes.

And it is one minute till the Quick Round by

my watch. And the clock on the wall. And everyone's clock, I think. I think I had better get out of here now. I pull hard. I kick. I yell. I watch the clock hands turn.

"*I have missed the Quick Round!*" Bang. Kick. Pound. Yell. "*I have missed the Quick Round!*" I figure this is just as good as yelling "Help!" And it makes me feel better. But only by a teeny, tiny bit.

Finally, finally I hear something.

"Hello?" someone calls from close by.

"HELLO!" I yell, pounding hard on the door.

"Ow!" says a voice from the other side. "What are you doing here?" Mom asks as she pushes open the door.

"Oh, just screaming and yelling and banging and trying to get out of a locked room!" I tell her.

"That's a good thing to do when you're in a locked room," she tells me. "Are you okay?"

"Yes."

"Do you know how this happened?"

"The door had a sign: 'Team Captains Meeting.' I went in. No one here but . . . ?"

"No sign on the door now," Mom tells me. "Are you okay?"

"I had a feeling," I tell her. "And yes, I'm okay."

"Someone is going to be in trouble about this." Mom bangs one fist into the other.

"The Quick Round?"

"Started."

"Jack?"

"Yes."

"Let's go."

Mom and I break the land speed record for school hallways. We screech round the corner to see Molly waiting by the door of room 113. And to see the door open, and the Sea Dragons file out. They don't look like happy, Boy Oh Boy Did We Do a Good Job, and Thank Goodness We Had Jack with Us Sea Dragons.

"I couldn't think of anything else to do," Jack is insisting.

"Anything else?" Timmy asks. In not the friendliest of voices.

"Remember, we're a team," Molly tells the Sea Dragons. "We stick together."

"What happened?" I ask.

"They gave us two paper plates," Mad Dog says.

"I made big mouse ears." Murphy holds up her hands behind her head.

"Mad Dog made a cool butterfly by folding them, and I made them into a sandwich." Timmy pretends to munch. "And Jack kept saying 'paper plate' and eating off them."

"I did that twice. I needed to do something," Jack says.

"He did something all right. He ripped them up," Timmy tells us.

"Ripped them up?" Molly asks.

"The plates. He ripped them up," Timmy repeats.

"At least it was just when time was up," Murphy admits.

"I couldn't think of anything else to do," Jack says. Again.

"Ripped them up?" Molly says.

"I threw them up into the air," Jack reports. "I started to say 'It's no use,' but the buzzer sounded."

A voice comes over the PA system: "All teams please report to the cafeteria for the results of today's competition."

Chapter Eight
Give That Boy a Prize

The judges and the Luderino sit behind a long table at the front of the room. They seem to be arguing about the piles of paper in front of them. The Luderino does not look happy.

Vikings, moose, sharks, army men, all the riders on the Imagination Railroad sit on either side of a wide aisle up the middle.

"For the ceremonial run of the winners," the head Viking man tells us.

"What are we going to do?" Mom asks Molly. "We can't just let this go. I'm going to go over to that Luderino and tell her exactly what happened. And exactly what is going to happen when I get my hands on the person who did this."

"What exactly happened, do you think?" Molly asks.

"I think someone tricked Conor so that he wouldn't be in the Quick Round." Mom looks around the room as if she has X-ray eyes that will tell her who it was.

"Then we have to do something now, or it will seem like sour grapes if we don't win," Molly points out.

"We're not going to win?" Jack asks.

"We have a chance," Molly tells us. "The play was great. We just don't know your other score."

"That's because they're still counting the little pieces of ripped paper plates," Timmy says.

"I don't think we should do anything," I tell Mom and Molly. A little quietly.

"Why not?" Mom starts that hand to fist hitting thing.

"Freaky Joe's Rule Number Four C," I say even more quietly.

"Oh," says Molly.

"Well, I don't know," says Mom.

"We have the results of today's wonderful competition," Ralfaella Luderino says. She stands up, waves a piece of paper.

The crowd yells "Imagination Railroad! Imagination Railroad!" Most of the crowd anyway.

"Let's just wait, okay?" I ask.

"You were all wonderful," the Luderino tells us. "But alas, only five teams can go on to the next round. These teams will proudly represent you all. And all of you can learn from their example of hard work and creative thinking. So please offer your congratulations to: The Cameron Toy Elementary School Vikings."

The Vikings leap to their feet. Give a Viking

cheer that sounds something like, "Oooogh aaah! Oooogh aaah!" They stomp their way up to the front.

"The Brendan Spears Spartans." These words send the green army people marching up front. Where they are joined by the Chammas Family Elementary School Moose Pack.

"The Lorne Duncan Elementary School Pyramids," she says next. "And finally, the team with the highest score, the winners of today's competition—the Edith R. Hammerrocker Elementary School Sea Dragons!"

"Yes!" I yell. We all yell.

The Luderino doesn't look as happy as we are. She looks like she just ate a lemon.

One of the judges takes the microphone.

"Look, that's the guy from our Quick Round." Murphy points.

"The Sea Dragons have the highest score, I am pleased to announce, because of both their teamwork, and one special team member. It does not often happen but today I am pleased to award a Wilhelmina Winkledorf Award!"

"A Winkledorf?"

"A Winkledorf!"

The word buzzes through the crowd. The Vikings all point at our team shouting "You! You! You!"

But who?

"Railroad Riders join me in congratulating the Hammerrocker Sea Dragons and Jack Bailey! Winner of the Wilhelmina Winkledorf Award for his completely creative work in the Quick Round. This original thinker shredded the paper plates. He threw them into the air, and yelled, 'Snow!' What a creative boy is this Jack."

Jack?

"Jack?" yells our team.

"Jack!" yells Jack.

An hour later, we are still at the school, with Mom still trying to round everyone up so we can go home. Every time it looks like we're ready to go, Jack wanders off to tell someone else the story of winning the Winkledorf. Even though everyone in the school already knows.

He also insists that he meant all along to say "snow."

"You said it yourself, Jack," Timmy points out again as we carry the Kingdom of the Dump to the back door. "You said 'It's no use.' The judge only heard 'It's no' because the buzzer went off."

"I was saying 'it's no use, I have no choice but to use my wonderful, original, creative idea to turn the plate into snow.'" Jack has his story and he's sticking to it.

"I need more candy if I have to listen to this on the ride home." Timmy heads to the concession stand.

"Did you see my medal, Conor?" Jack holds it up for the 1,523rd time.

"It's great, Jack."

"I wonder if that man over there sweeping the

floor has seen it." Jack heads over to share it with the custodian for the fourteenth time.

"Way to go, Sea Dragons," the Viking coach calls as he heads out the door.

"Wait!" I realize I've forgotten an important question.

"Sure, what can I do for you?" the coach asks, taking off his horned helmet. Which turns out to have his hair attached to it. Maybe he should keep it on.

"Did your team get an envelope delivered during lunch break?" I ask. "By one of the green soldiers?"

"Sure, we got that schedule for the next competition. Did you lose your copy?" He reaches inside his fur Viking vest and pulls out a crumpled piece of paper. "Do you want to copy it?"

"No, I'll just remember the date and tell my mom," I say, handing it back. I'll tell my mom all right. Tell her that it looks like the team captain meeting may have been for our team only.

"Oooogh aaah," the Vikings call as they go.

"Back at you," I tell them.

"Exciting, isn't it?" I jump a little at the question. I didn't hear the Luderino come up behind me.

"Exciting." I agree with her.

"Your friend is proud of his award." She points at Jack, who is now sharing it with a security guard.

"That's a good thing," I say. Why is she talking to me?

"But did he deserve it? From our first meeting, I would have said you were one of the best Quick Round players—that you were more likely to win a Willie, Conor. It is Conor, isn't it?" the Luderino asks.

"Yup, Conor. And I think Jack deserved it."

Okay, so I crossed my fingers. I didn't like her asking that about Jack.

"Conor what? I didn't get your last name? Is it McGuire?" she asks me.

"McGuire? It's not McGuire. That's my coach's last name."

"That's right, Molly McGuire. Are you Valerie's son?"

"Miz Barnes of the Big Blue Bookstore?" I ask her. "Why would you think she's my mom?"

"My mistake, so sorry." The Luderino tilts her head as she looks at me. Which reminds me of Riley, when she's thinking. "Yes, you must be Maura's son. Yes, that would make sense."

"Huh?" I ask her. "Why are you asking about my mom?"

"Just being polite, sonny. I like to know everything I can about those who ride my railroad.

Well, I must be off. Till we meet again." She does that strange, finger wave at me.

Strange. That's the word all right. For just about everything that has happened this afternoon.

Strange.

Chapter Nine

Oh Tell Us, Tell Us, Jack Man

The next morning, while Bella is jumping up and down the stairs two feet at a time, my mom says, "Freaky Joe's Rule Number Four C?"

I state the rule. "Don't say who did it, if you don't know who did it."

"I know the rule, dearie. I was only going to say what happened, not who did it. But then that Luderino started talking, and Jack won, and I never got to do it."

"Okay, wrong rule. Maybe Rule Number Seventeen C?" I better go check Rule Number Seventeen C.

"Let's forget the rules and figure out who did

it," Mom suggests. "Do you think it could be your old friend Jeremiah? He's smart enough to know you were better than him." She has a point.

"But where did he get the key? You found a key in the lock when you opened the door."

"So you think someone sent you a note to go to the meeting, waited till you were in the room, and then locked the door behind you? To keep you from the Quick Round? Because you're the best one on our team?"

"Sounds dumb?" I ask.

"Sounds like what happened," she answers. "Sounds like you'd better figure out why someone doesn't want you to win."

"Sounds like a job for the Freaky Joe Club," I admit.

"What's the plan?"

"The Condor aims to start by finding out who

has been listening outside the Secret Place," I tell her. "That's the Condor's plan."

And later that day, in the cafeteria, I put my plan into action.

"After school today. In the Secret Place. Important meeting," I tell Timmy.

"I thought we had practice tomorrow?" he asks as he eats the first of his three sandwiches.

"We do. This is Freaky stuff."

"On the job." Timmy stops eating long enough to salute.

"Jack," I start to say.

"Oh, I know, you need some help from me about something, don't you." Jack says this in a loud voice. "It's hard when you've won a Winkledorf. Everyone always wants your help with everything." He wears the Winkledorf medal, the big brass circle on a green ribbon, around his neck.

"Winkledorf?" Gavin, a roller hockey player, asks. "Is that a disease?"

"The fact that you don't know what it is, is a sign that you cannot have won one," Jack explains. Or confuses. "Do you want me to show you how to open that bag of pretzels? Award winners know how to do these things."

"Jack?" I whisper, loudly.

"Excuse me," he says to another kid. "I'll tell you the best way to open a milk carton after I assist my friend here."

"Important club business. I need you to come to the Secret Place after school," I explain.

"Of course you do," Jack says, as he pats me on the back. "Of course you need me."

Oh boy.

During recess, I put the next part of my plan into action.

"We'll have Imagination Railroad practice after school today. Around four o'clock," I say. Just loud enough so that some people can hear me. And some others cannot.

"So what's the deal?" Timmy asks as he barrels into the room.

"I have a plan," I answer. "And we have a mystery to solve."

"Like why would anyone give Jack an award?" Timmy asks. "Here you go, buddy," he tells Bob as he feeds him from a little bag labeled Chocolate Hamster Chunks.

"Why someone delivered a fake note to our team. Was the plan to make me miss the Quick Round? And why?"

"Or was it some big mistake?" Timmy suggests. "And not about us. Or you?"

"The door was open when I went in," I remind him. "And then locked on the outside with a key."

"Okay, that's a big clue," Timmy decides. He pulls a lollipop out of his pocket. "Time to think."

"Time to think?" Jack asks as he comes through the door. "Then it is a good thing that I, Jack, winner of the Wilhelmina Winkledorf Award, am here." He stands there, arms wide, medal shining in the sun.

Riley growls. Bob starts throwing wood shavings.

"Good thing," I say. "Now here's the plan."

It is a well-known fact that the one thing Sea Dragons are very,

very good at is hiding. (It's well-known to any-one who knows anything about Sea Dragons.) They swim up against coral, around sea plants, and they simply cannot be seen. Like me, right now, outside the Secret Place, behind two garbage cans, and a large green plant. At least I hope.

I hear the voices.

"I'm telling you, Jack, this trick will make sure we win the next competition." Timmy says. Loudly.

"I think I know best about this, Timmy." Jack's turn. "You may not remember, but I've won an award. . . ."

I hope this doesn't take hours. I don't know how long Timmy can hold out.

"No, Jack, I didn't know you won an award. Was it for the strangest answer ever given in a round?"

"Oh no," Jack answers.

"Was it a special award for people who destroy the props?" Timmy wonders.

I raise my head to peek out. Aha! I was right. Go, Conor, go, Conor, I do a little mental end zone dance. Go Riley, go Riley, I think as I stand up and blow hard on my whistle. Which causes the person who was

outside the window listening, to stand up and begin to run.

Which causes Timmy to quickly open the door of the Secret Place. Which frees Riley, The Beast of the Freaky Joe Club.

"Go get him, girl," Timmy yells. "He's got lots of treats."

Riley runs. Jumps. Lands.

"Hold him, girl!" I yell. "I'm coming."

"Get this monster off of me," Jeremiah yells. Riley sits on his back, happily licking his head. Timmy says this guy has treats. Riley believes Timmy.

"Not yet, not until you answer one or two questions," I tell Jeremiah.

"I would actually be the perfect person to answer your questions," Jack interrupts.

"Timmy, would you ask Jack to go inside and

begin work on that other special project?" I give Timmy a look that says, "Please?"

"Special project." Timmy salutes.

"That sounds perfect for me," Jack tells him as they walk away. "I don't know if I reminded you but I won . . ."

"That is really and truly awful," Jeremiah says. At least I think that's what he says. It's a little hard to hear him with his face in the grass.

"Why are you spying on us?" I ask.

"I'm not," he says.

"Are too," I tell him. Which doesn't exactly sound like big-deal spy talk. "This is the third time. The first two times you had someone else along. One voice said to the other, 'They're doing something with straws.' The next time you said, 'I think they're doing something in space.' And then your play was about aliens."

"It was a lousy play," he admits.

"It was," I said. "But that made it funny."

"It wasn't supposed to be funny," Jeremiah tells the grass. "Your dog is heavy," he tells me.

"Tell me why you were spying and I'll get her off," I promise.

"Call her off, and I'll tell you," Jeremiah counters.

I don't think so. "No."

"I wanted us to win, and I had no idea how to do it," Jeremiah confesses.

"Will you really stay?" I ask.

"Yup."

"Riley, good girl," I tell her. "Go jump on Jack." Riley tilts her head to one side to let me know she understands. Then she turns, runs to the Secret Place, and jumps up, hitting the door with her top two paws.

"Smart dog," Jeremiah says.

"Sometimes," I say.

"Noooooooo!" Jack yells from inside.

"So," I ask as Jeremiah wipes the grass off.

"So, the Sharks always win," he begins.

"Mostly win," I remind him.

"Mostly always win," Jeremiah admits, "because we're better than the other teams. In Sylvan Glen, we work at winning. Practice, practice, practice. Our moms and dads really want us to win. So they help us. And make us practice, practice, practice.

105

But no one was interested in helping us with this stuff. It wasn't a sport, or anything, so they didn't get it."

"So you didn't know what you were doing?" I get it. "But why bother?" I ask. "Why ride the Railroad?"

"'Cause you were going to win. So I wanted to beat you. And," Jeremiah looks around, then shrugs his shoulders.

"And, what?" I ask.

"And it sounded, I don't know, different." Jeremiah looks like this is hard for him to admit. "My next-door neighbor, Miss Willie, told me all about it. She made it sound interesting. Even fun."

"So you decided to copy us?" I ask. Miss Willie?

"Learn from you," Jeremiah admits. "Big Buster may know hockey, but he wasn't a very good coach for this."

"Why did you come back today? The Sharks were eliminated."

Jeremiah looks around, like he's checking if someone will hear him. "'Cause I'm still interested. Even if none of the other Sharks are."

"Thanks," I tell him.

"For what?" Jeremiah asks.

"Telling me the truth," I answer.

"I could beat you bad," Jeremiah says, "if I knew what I was doing." Standing, he wipes the grass off.

"Not with that play, you couldn't," I tell him.

An amazing thing happens that has never happened before: Jeremiah grins. "No, not with that play. And you are amazing at Quick Round."

Now that's amazing. That he would say it.

"One last question?" I ask. "Did you lock me in the storage room so I couldn't compete in the Quick Round?"

"Huh?" He looks completely confused.

"Never mind," I tell him.

"You can be weird. But never as weird as Jack," he tells me.

"See ya," I say to Jeremiah as he grabs his bike from the front of the garage.

"When I beat you," he calls as he rides away.

Miss Willie?

Chapter Ten

Take a Look, Take a Look in a Book

After asking myself the same question all night, in the morning I have an idea. Of where to go to find the answer.

I grab my bicycle and head to the school. To the library.

Miss Hoopes, the librarian, is busy unpacking a box of books.

"New books," she says. "Unread. Waiting for all of us to open them." She holds one up for me to see. "Can there be anything more exciting?"

I agree with her. "Not much."

"Do you come seeking information or entertainment?" she asks.

"Today, information. Old information," I tell her.

"*A History of Prater County from Then Till Now*?" she asks. She knows that book held an important clue that solved another case.

"Nope. How about a history of the Edith R. Hammerrocker School?" I wonder if there is such a thing.

"Ah, a tougher question. I love it." Miss Hoopes leaps to her feet and dusts her hands together. "Follow me to wisdom," she says.

She leads me around to the back of the library. Where there is a tall bookcase filled with videos, magazines, and big books that look sort of like photo albums.

"Videos of talent shows since we first had a video camera," she points to the top shelves. "Next we have copies of the *Hammerrocker How-About-It*, our magazine of student writing. And here"—Miss Hoopes pulls one of those big books out—" we have the scrapbooks for each year." She blows dust off the top. "At least since they started keeping scrapbooks," she says.

I wonder if I'm lucky enough.

"Do you have these years?" I show her the numbers I copied off the plaque.

"Here's one." She pulls out a fat, dusty book with papers sticking out all the edges.

"I'll set you up at this table here," Miss Hoopes puts the book down at a table in the back. "Take your time; be careful of old paper— it rips easily. Call me when you're finished"— she pauses for a breath—"and tell me what you find. Because the last time we did this, you came up with a doozy."

"I will," I promise, "take my time, be careful, and tell you if I find something."

I turn the big pages of the scrapbook carefully. It's funny to think that all these kids are grown-ups now. Are as old as, well, my mom. And they probably have kids that they tell to go to bed, and wash their hands, and do their homework. But when the pictures in the scrapbook were taken, I bet they never thought they'd say that when they grew up.

"Please be in here," I whisper. I want to be right. I don't know what I want to be right about. But I want there to be a clue in this book.

And here's the page I want. Old newspaper pictures of five girls smiling at the camera. It's a

little funny to look at them, but the names tell me I'm right.

And then there is the picture next to it.

Bingo. This is what I was hoping to see. The other kids. The other team. Three girls and two

boys. Willie? Yes! There she is. But who are the other kids?

Oh.

Oh ho.

This falls under the category of Big Time Interesting.

I think I might know why a door was locked behind me. And why someone's face looked like it had eaten a lemon. I think.

But I think I know where I have to go to find out if I'm right.

So this afternoon finds me on my bicycle. I ride down Ship's Cove Boulevard, with trees on my left and houses on my right. I'm heading toward the hole in the fence, the one that leads to the back way into Sylvan Glen.

I pass Bubba Butowski, our ace security guard, who spends his days making sure the dogs of Ship's Cove are happy. Right now he has our Riley and Rosie the greyhound in the front seat of the Ship's Cove Security Service truck. It looks awfully crowded. The dogs look completely happy. Riley eats a dog biscuit and Rosie appears to be eating Riley's ear.

"Hey, hey, Bubba," I call out.

"Hey, hey, Conor," he calls back. I see him turn into The Lime in the Coconut Lane. Three dogs wait there, on the corner. As soon as they see Bubba, they all lift their front paws, moaning. That'll be good for a free ride and a biscuit.

I keep going. I find the hole in the brick wall between our two neighborhoods. I speed up past the house of the lady who throws candy corn. Checking the street numbers, I find the right house. Next to Jeremiah's. I park my bicycle, take a deep breath. And ring the bell.

And she answers it. And I ask her name.

After that we talk.

And I'm almost there. Freaky Joe would be proud of me.

Chapter Eleven

And the Sea Dragons Sing

"Molly said it was a good idea. It's a good idea," my mom says. She says "It's a good idea" for the one-hundredth time.

But I'm still not buying it.

Okay, my little sister looks extremely cute dressed as a Sea Dragon. She has a Sea Dragon hat on her head, and the shapes of ocean plants all over her. "And the other three are dressed the same?" I ask. The other three are the evil genius Mugsy, her little brother, Mikey, and his best friend, Dwayne.

"Different colors. I had a wonderful time on that Web site you found. Sea Dragons must be some of the most beautiful and unusual creatures in the sea." Mom starts to go dreamy on me, waving her brush in the air.

"The costumes are great. I'm glad you had fun making them. But I thought we were trying to win by doing well, not because we're wearing goofy costumes."

"You're not wearing a goofy costume," Mom points out. "Bella is."

"It's not goofy. It's beautiful," Bella insists.

"But we could lose all our points when Mugsy and company rush the stage during our play."

"Nonsense," Mom says. "I'll have control of them at all times."

"Sea Dragons, Sea Dragons,
Sea Dragons Rule.
They come from the Hammerrocker
Elementary School."

Bella does a great cheer.

Molly pulls up with her car. The other Sea Dragons get dropped off. Murphy arrives with Mugsy, Mikey, and Dwayne. I hate to admit it, but the little guys all look way cool as Sea Dragons. And they still don't look as weird as Mr. Head Viking.

We drive along singing songs about Sea Dragons. We sing tunes we know, but we change the words.

"You ain't nothing but a Sea Dragon,
crying all the time.
You ain't never caught a starfish
and you ain't no fish of mine."

• • • •

The same wild scene greets us. Only it is more wild. More teams. More costumes. "I was told we should set up shop in the cafeteria," Molly says. "Grab a table, set up for the day."

We head in, dragging the Kingdom of the Dump in boxes and bags, a cooler full of food and drink that Timmy has inspected three times, and four small Sea Dragons who jump and hop like they are kangaroos instead of extraordinary creatures of the deep. Mom carries a sign on a stick.

"This will sit in the middle of our table," she says.

SEA DRAGONS RULE!
UNDER THE SEA, HERE,
OR IN SCHOOL.

We are good to go for an exciting day on the Imagination Railroad. All should be well.

Unless you know what I know.

And then, you've got to wonder.

Will she try again to stop me?

Our Quick Round is our first round this time. Mom stays in the cafeteria, chasing the little Sea Dragons who forgot that coming to cheer meant spending the day behaving at one table.

Room 224 this time. We walk together. Nothing happens to any of us. Jack and Molly sit in the two chairs outside the door. We march in, bang fists together.

"Sea Dragons Rule," we tell the judge.

"One red straw and a plastic cup," she says. "I am setting the timer now."

We do okay. Come up with ideas, pass the straw and cup.

No one says "straw" or "cup."

My favorite was when Timmy stuck the cup over his mouth, held the straw to the end. "Pig eating licorice," he said. Said once we were able to pull the stuck cup off his face.

Ralfaella Luderino seems to be everywhere. And everywhere she is, the teams sing or dance or act weird, so she'll notice them. Since she can give lots and lots of extra points, is this really such a bad idea?

Well, yes, it is.

"Two more rounds and we do our play," Molly announces. "Let's go get ready."

"You are allowed to watch this and cheer," Mom tells the small sea creatures. "Anyone found swimming away or interfering with the play will not be happy."

The competition is taking place in the Helen McMullin High School, so we get to do the play on the fancy high school stage.

Leaving our cheering squad, we head backstage to get ready.

We put on our costumes. Paint Jack's face gray. With all our props ready and the wagon good to go, we watch the team before us. Who are busy trying to bring a box of chocolate to life. I'm watching the play, but I still can't figure out why.

"Five minutes," Molly says.

I look outside. See little Sea Dragons. And, surprise, a big Jeremiah sitting next to the other person I was hoping to see.

"Great job, teams, great job." Ralfaella moves through the backstage area, congratulating everyone, being really nice.

Maybe I was wrong. Maybe nothing will happen. I'm safe, and all is well.

"Next team is the Edith R. Hammerrocker Sea Dragons," the judge announces.

Jack climbs into his wagon. The bell rings.

Timmy, Murphy, Mad Dog, and I run out. We quickly set our scene. Murphy starts dancing around and Timmy pretends to cook in a plastic can while I tidy up the old books.

"Pssst," Mad Dog calls from off stage. "Pssst."

I look over to where he stands off stage. "No Jack!" he says.

"No Jack," I say out loud. Oh no! Jack. Winner of the Winkledorf. Of course.

Murphy and Timmy look confused. "No Jack?"

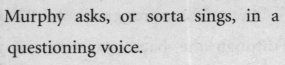

Murphy asks, or sorta sings, in a questioning voice.

"That's right," I sing back. "Somehow we have no Jack!" Hoping someone will hear us. And help.

I look out into the audience. Mom shakes her head.

"Oh what can we do without a Jack!" Timmy sings. "I cannot make my sauce without a Jack."

The back doors of the auditorium are open. I see him! Jack is pointing at us, jumping up and down. Ralfaella Luderino is showing him a piece of paper, pulling his arm and pointing in the other direction!

"Look, everyone, look!" I sing as loud as I can.

Sorta of a mix of sing and shout. "There is our Jack! We have found our Jack!"

"Jack, oh Jack!" Timmy and Murphy sing.

"Everyone help us," I cry. "Call to our Jack."

The audience begins to laugh. Jack begins to wave. The little Sea Dragons stand on their chairs. "Jack, oh Jack," they call. "Why is that lady taking our Jack?"

Jack pulls away, runs down the aisle.

"Jack, here is our Jack," the audience sings.

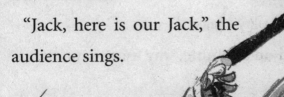

"I am Jack," Jack sings. "The award-winning Jack!" He runs up on the stage, bowing to everyone. They clap. Jack bows. They clap again. Jack bows again.

We could be here all day.

But what about our play? Our time is almost up and we haven't started.

The bell rings. The judge calls, "Time."

Ralfaella Luderino comes back in the auditorium. "That was time," she calls to us. "Can we have the next play please?"

"Now hold on a minute," my mom says, standing up.

"They didn't do their play," Molly insists.

"They didn't?" says the judge. "Then what was that?"

"That is what they'll be scored on," Ralfaella says.

"That is someone trying to stop us from doing our play, so we can't win," I say. In a loud voice.

"Don't be ridiculous, little boy." Ralfaella looks most annoyed. "Next play, please."

"I don't think so," calls Mom as she reaches the stage. She's rolling up her sleeves. Not good.

And she's not the only one standing up. Yes!

"I don't think so, either." The lady I had been looking for walks over to Ralfaella. "That'll be enough, Ralphie," she says.

"Ralphie?" my mom shouts. "Ralphie!"

"You're Ralphie?" Molly shouts from the stage. "Ralphie?"

"Girlfriend, you are looking good," Mom says.

"What's going on?" asks the judge.

"Just a little reunion of old friends," Miss Willie says. "Right, Ralphie? You're going to let them do their play."

"My name is Ralfaella Luderino," Ralphie says. "They may do their play," she tells her. "But I don't know how they'll score."

"How about I help you figure that out?" Mom wants to know.

How about no? Luckily, a small Sea Dragon takes that moment to try and escape. Mom runs after. Willie takes a seat.

And we do our play. A statue of Good King Bob comes to the Kingdom of the Dump. Where he is rescued, brought back to life, and marches on.

The audience loves our play, clapping and cheering. Well, the sea creature part of the audience.

Chapter Twelve

So What's in a Name?

"I still can't believe it," Mom tells Molly as we sit around the Sea Dragon table. "I cannot believe Ralphie Vitali is Ralfaella Luderino."

"She told me I had to go be interviewed by a television station right away," Jack tells us what had been going on. "Because I won the Winkledorf, they wanted to talk to me."

"Clever plan," I say.

"I thought it was important that I be on TV. I have won a Winkledorf award, you know," Jack reminds us. "She said you would wait for me."

"Ralphie?" Timmy asks. "Ralphie is the Luderino?"

"Her name was—is—Ralfaella," Molly explains.

"Nobody ever called her anything but Ralphie, so we just forgot."

"So she was on the other team?" Timmy asks. "When you won the competition?"

"That's right," Mom tells all of us. "Ralphie was on the Sharks and we were the Mermaids. And we won."

"But it was so, so close," I add. "Very close."

"Who's a clever boy?" Mom asks.

"You've been reading again, haven't you, Conor?" Jack asks.

"I went to the old scrapbooks at school. They had newspaper cuttings from the stories about the two teams. It was interesting stuff," I tell them.

"And Ralphie?" Molly asks.

"There was her picture in the newspaper. Along with Willie," I report.

"So Luderino must be her married name?" Murphy suggests.

"Must be," Molly says.

"But Conor, Ralphie didn't look *anything* like she does now," Mom points out.

"Anything," Molly echoes. "That's why we kept thinking we knew her, but didn't know how."

I have to agree that the girl in the newspaper clipping, the big girl with the big hair, big teeth, big braces, and big glasses looks nothing like the Luderino does today.

"Her name," I tell them. "The newspaper printed Ralfaella, not Ralphie. The pieces fit. It had to be her."

"That's fine detective work," Mom says.

"Well, there's a lot of detectives here," Timmy adds. He's eating something pink and—and silver?

"And one Winkledorf winner," Jack reminds everyone again.

"And Wilhelmina Winkledorf was on that same team, wasn't she?" I look at Mom and Molly.

"My Wilhelmina?" Jack cries.

"Yours," I tell him. "She was on the Sharks with Ralphie. And she scored the highest points ever scored by one person in the Quick Round. But it wasn't enough to win. Because Ralphie was pretty bad at it. And Mom and Molly's team was really good. They scored more points overall."

"So they created the Winkledorf Award to honor me," says the lady from the audience as she and Jeremiah walk up to our table.

"Willie!" Mom and Molly jump up.

"Shark!" Jack yells. He and the small Sea Dragons dive under the table.

Timmy keeps eating pink stuff.

I say "Hey" to Jeremiah.

He nods back.

"Even though our team didn't win, I did get an award named after me. Which was good enough for me," Willie says.

"But Ralphie didn't get an award," I point out.

"No, she didn't," Willie says. "We may have to do something about Ralphie."

"I have an idea." Mom does that Hand Hitting Her Other Hand thing.

"Will all teams please report to the auditorium for the award ceremony," says the voice over the PA.

There's not enough room in the auditorium for everyone. People, and creatures, are sitting everywhere.

"Leave a center aisle, leave a center aisle

clear." A judge keeps walking up and down.

On the stage, a table has been set up with awards. The judges line up behind it.

The Luderino takes the microphone.

"What a great day this has been," Ralfaella begins. "It has been almost impossible to choose the best team. But we have had to do it. Two teams will leave here and go on to the state competition. We will cheer them on and wish them well."

Another judge interrupts, which does not make the Luderino look happy. "But before we do that, there is someone very, very special here today. Would everyone give a warm, Imagination Railroad welcome to Wilhelmina Winkledorf herself!"

Miss Willie stands up and waves. The crowd claps and waves. Jack stands on a chair, holding out his medal.

"Exciting, isn't it?" Ralfaella says in a Not Excited at All voice.

"And now, the judges will hand me the scores. Be brave, everyone." The Luderino takes the scores. Opens them. Frowns. Looks over at the judges. Looks out at the audience. Frowns.

"One moment, please." She walks back over to the judges. Much whispering and pointing at papers.

The audience whispers and hums.

She comes back to the microphone. "Thank you for your patience. And the winner is: The Alex Tee Elementary School Wizards.

"Please come on down front and receive your prizes," Ralfaella Luderino says.

"Shazam!" The Wizards jump and yell their way to the stage.

"There are supposed to be two winners," Molly calls out. Loudly.

"Who's the second winner?" Mom yells.

"There's a problem with the scoring. A question of whether to allow some points," The Luderino answers. "I am sorry, but we will have to let the second team know at a later point."

"That's not fair!" someone yells. Okay, *I* yell.

"I am the conductor of the Imagination Railroad, Western division, and I will decide what's fair." The Luderino does not look happy.

"I believe we should give the Sea Dragons their prize," one of the judges says.

"I believe you should sit there and be nice and quiet," the Luderino shouts.

Oops.

"Sea Dragons! Sea Dragons! Sea Dragons!" the

little kids start to chant. Molly and Mom stand up and start to chant. I can't figure out if it is cool or embarrassing.

"Thank you all for coming, this meeting is over!" The Luderino bangs on the microphone.

"Hey, where's our prize?" the Wizard coach asks.

"You'll get your prize when I say so!" The Luderino grabs the Wizard's tall

hat with the stars and moons on it. And hits her over the head with it!

"Everyone go home!" Ralfaella screams.

"Sea Dragons! Sea Dragons!" we all chant.

"Prizes! Prizes!" the Wizards yell.

The Luderino and the Wizard coach are fighting over the hat.

"Ralphie! Ralphie!" a voice cries louder through the noise.

"DON'T CALL ME THAT!"

This gets everyone's attention.

Wilhelmina Winkledorf takes the stage. "Then stop acting like the kid we used to call Ralphie," Willie says. "She was always a sore loser," she tells the audience. "We lost to the Hammerrocker Mermaids, and she cried for two weeks straight. And stopped eating."

"That part seems to have been good," Mom tells Molly.

"Stopped eating!" Timmy yells in a horrified voice.

"We were cheated!" Ralphie yells.

"You were no good at the Quick Round," Willie tells her. "You just kept saying 'straw?' over and over."

"We were cheated!" Ralphie yells. "But Willie still had an award named for her. I had nothing. But I promised myself when I grew up, I would change things."

"I've promised myself when I grow up I'm going to eat a whole bowl of cake batter without making the cake," Bella tells Mugsy.

"And I did! I am head of this Railroad. And at my competitions, even if you're no good at Quick Round, you can still win! You can win by being nice to me! If you dress like a fool, and wear a ridiculous hat, you can win because you did that for me! So I would notice you and say, 'Yes!' You can win because I want you to! Isn't that so much better?"

The Luderino spreads her arms wide, asking the question of a room full of people in silly hats and foolish clothing.

Willie Winkledorf takes the microphone away. "Well, she asked the question. Is it better? Better than winning by using your imagination?"

Silence for a minute.

"Is this a test?" Jack whispers.

"No! No!" The Viking coach thunders his answer. He stands up. And throws his horns on the floor.

"No!"

"No!"

"Look at me, I look like an idiot with a frog on my head," a coach yells.

"I'm glad I didn't have to tell her that," Mom tells Molly.

The Luderino stands there, staring.

"And are you ready to announce the other winner of this competition?" Willie looks at the judges.

"The Sea Dragons!" the judges all yell.

"Sea Dragons Rule!" we chant as we head to the stage.

"No! No!" Ralphie finds her voice. "Their coaches are cheaters. They cheated me. They're trying to cheat you! I tried to stop them, I've tried to help all of you!"

"The Sea Dragons are the winners," the judges say again.

"Then I quit! You see what happens to this railroad when I quit!"

There's that quiet again for a minute. And then the audience breaks into cheers. Starts clapping. Stamping their feet. Singing a song that says, "Good-bye!"

And then Ralfaella Luderino, in her purple suit, with the purple feather collar, and the purple feather cuffs, puts her thumb on her nose. She wiggles her ring-covered fingers, sticks out her tongue and makes an awful noise. "That's what I say to you guys." She walks off the stage in a hurry. Breaking one of her high, high heels.

Chapter Thirteen

One Freaky Joe Club
+
One Freaky Joe Club

"Well, that was one interesting case," Molly announces as she cuts into a large cake. A cake in the shape of a Sea Dragon.

"And fun!" Jack says. "I just love that railroad. But it's easy to love things that one is so good at."

"No kidding, Medal Boy," Timmy tells him as he takes another piece of our Victory Cake.

"It was like a time travel case, like when Sir Chester and Chuck entered that mysterious cave and found themselves at a Red Sox baseball game." I loved that book.

"I know that story," Bella tells everyone while

she does a handstand. "Conor read me about Chuck hitting a house run."

"Home run," I remind her.

"I like this case best because we didn't have to write clues on pieces of paper," Jack says. "I always hate that part."

"But it always works," Mom says.

"But I didn't like it either," Molly admits.

"That's because you were always writing songs when you were supposed to be solving a mystery," Mom points out.

"Having a Winkledorf winner around will be a big help in solving mysteries. And I happen to have won a Winkledorf," Jack tells everyone.

Riley moans and covers her ears with her paws. Bob throws food at his cage wall.

"Did you ever run out of cases?" Timmy asks Mom.

"No, we ran out of being kids before we ran out of cases," she tells him.

"And then you waited for Conor to be old enough?"

"Correctomundo," Mom tells him. "That's what I was taught to do."

"Who taught you that?" Timmy asks.

"Her dad did," I answer for her.

"Aha, a new piece of information," Timmy says.

"And someone taught him," I add.

"You knew my club wasn't the first club, didn't you?" Mom asks.

"Yup. But now I know more," Timmy answers. "I shall have to think on this." He takes two dog biscuits out of his pocket, gives one to Riley, and begins to chew on one himself.

"Why don't we look at some of the Secret Files together," I suggest.

"Will you show us one that goes all the way back to Freaky Joe?" Timmy asks.

"You haven't seen her yet?" Molly asks.

"Her?" Jack asks.

"Freaky Joe is not a he? Aha!" Timmy says.

"He is she?" Jack looks worried.

"So Conor learned from his mother." Timmy points at me with the dog biscuit. "So his mother must have learned from . . ."

"Her mother," Jack exclaims. "Always ask a Winkledorf winner."

"Wrong," I tell him.

"Okay, she learned from her father," Timmy figures.

"Right," my mother answers.

"Sooooo, he learned from his mother. Is that where it starts?" Timmy asks.

"Yes. See here." Mom turns the book to the

beginning. "This is the first Freaky Joe Club. And this is Freaky Joe herself. . . ."

"My great-grandmother." I point to her.

"She doesn't look that old," Jack says.

"Why did she do it?" Timmy is Question Boy today.

"To have some fun," Mom answers. "And I think she wanted to show 'em. Back then girls were supposed to do lots of household chores, and maybe be more polite, not have the kind of wild fun boys could have. Mary Josephine didn't think that was fair. She wanted to do something interesting. And exciting. One day her brothers were talking about how no one could figure out who swiped Brian Daniels' mule. Mary Jo figured she could do it. She and her two best friends did. They put the mule back in his barn with a sign, 'Freaky Joe found him.' That was the beginning of the club."

"The mystery-solving club," I add. "And she kept a book about it."

"And when she grew up, she gave the book to her son," my mom finishes.

"And he to you, and you to Conor." Timmy chews the dog biscuit happily.

"The end," Jack announces.

"I don't think so," I tell him.

"I agree," Mom says.

"Will we have to remember this?" Jack asks.

"I thought you were Genius Boy," Timmy says.

"Well, I have won a Winkledorf," Jack begins.

"Aaarrgghh! I can't take it anymore!" Timmy throws himself through the air. Onto Jack.

Jack goes down.

Riley jumps on Timmy.

"Aaarrgghh! I'm being crushed!" Jack cries. "Someone save me."

"Think of an amazing plan to save yourself, Smart Boy," Timmy tells him.

"Come here, Riley girl." I wave a bone at her. This always works.

"We are the little Sea Dragons who eat the bigger dragons," Mugsy yells as she throws herself on Timmy and Jack. Followed closely by Bella, Mikey, and Dwayne.

"Then I'll just be the Coach Who Eats Cake," Molly says.

"And I'll be the mother who wants to look at the Secret Files with her son." Mom steps over the large pile of kids wrestling on the floor.

And I still am The Condor. Solver of mysteries.
Leader of this Freaky Joe Club. And friend to my
friends. To all mystery-reading, mystery-solving
friends. Wherever they are.